Wendy
and the Surprise Party

Illustrations by Craig Cameron and Pulsar

EGMONT

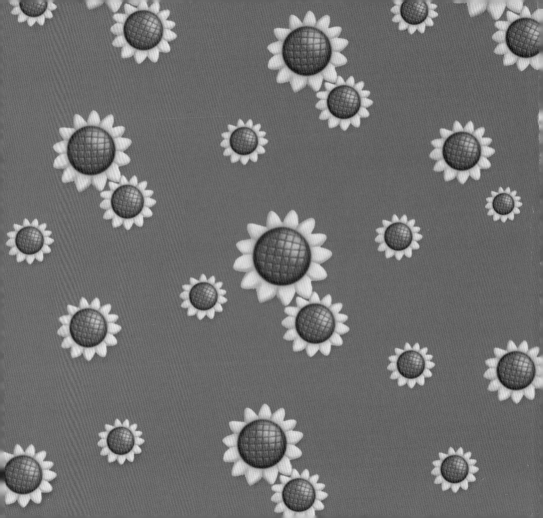

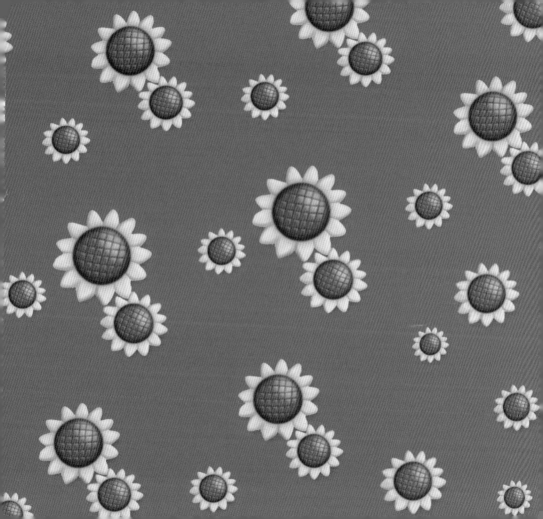

EGMONT

We bring stories to life

First published in Great Britain 2007
This edition published in 2010
by Egmont UK Limited,
239 Kensington High Street, London W8 6SA
Endpapers and introductory illustrations by Craig Cameron.

HiT entertainment

ISBN 978 1 4052 3140 4

1 3 5 7 9 10 8 6 4 2

Printed in Malaysia

When Wendy planned a surprise party for Bob, she had to organise the dome building work at the same time! Would Wendy be able to do both?

In Sunflower Valley, Bob and the team were building a dome.

"You've done a great job getting all the parts, Wendy," said Bob. "So I think you should be in charge."

"Oh Bob, I'd love to!" replied Wendy. But then she began to look worried.

As Bob walked away, Wendy whispered to the machines:

"I need you to help me keep Bob busy. I'm planning a surprise party for him tomorrow night at the dome! Mr Bentley is letting everyone know."

"But the dome isn't built yet!" cried Muck.

Wendy wasn't worried about building the dome. But she was worried about how she was going to organise the party! Bob and the machines were ready to start.

"Can we build it?" asked Scoop.

"Yes we can!" replied the machines.

"Er . . . yeah, I think so," added Lofty.

They dug the foundations and made a timber frame.

Then Scrambler whizzed in with
Mr and Mrs Bentley.

"Hello, everybody!" said Mr Bentley.
"We are here to pick a spot for our
new house!"

"We're going to live in a tent while
we build it," added Mrs Bentley.

"I'll show you where to pitch it," offered
Wendy. But she was really leaving so she
could organise the party!

Wendy had just picked up her phone when Scoop arrived.

"Can you come back and tell Bob what to do next?" asked Scoop.

"Bernard will help you with the party tonight," said Mrs Bentley.

"Tonight?" replied Wendy. "But the party is tomorrow!"

Mr Bentley had told everyone to come on the wrong night! Wendy decided that she would organise the party when she got back from the building site.

"We've got to be quick or it won't be finished in time," said Wendy, when she saw Bob and Dizzy stood looking at the dome pieces.

"In time for what?" asked Bob.

"Oh, nothing Bob!" replied Wendy,

Soon the first layer of the dome was complete. Wendy decided to sneak away to make the phone calls about the party.

"Wendy, what do we need to do next?" asked Bob.

"Just look at my notes," called Wendy. "It's all in there!" And then she zoomed away on Muck, leaving Bob looking confused.

Wendy arrived at her mobile home and found the Bentleys there.

"I'm just calling Mrs Percival," said Mr Bentley.

"Oh, I'll talk to her," said Wendy, nervously.

Just then, Farmer Pickles arrived with everyone from Bobsville, including Mrs Percival! Wendy was worried that Bob might see them.

But Wendy and Muck had to go back to the site.

"You get back to the dome and we'll sort out everything for the party," said Mr Bentley.

"Oh no, I can deal with it," said Wendy. "Don't do anything, Mr Bentley. I will be back soon."

At the site, Wendy soon saw that Bob hadn't left space for the doors into the dome!

"Oops, I'll just have to start this layer again!" said Bob.

"But that will take too long!" said Wendy.

"Wendy, why don't you let Mr Bentley organise the party?" whispered Muck. "You can't organise the dome and the party at the same time."

Just then, Scrambler zoomed in with Mr Bentley.

"Oh, Mr Bentley, I'm sorry I wouldn't let you help," said Wendy, looking at Muck. "Can you organise the party?"

"I would be delighted!" replied Mr Bentley, and Scrambler zoomed off!

With the team working together, the dome was soon finished. Bob went to his mobile home to get some cordial to celebrate.

But when he returned, the dome was decorated with balloons and everyone was wearing party hats!

"Surprise!" cried the Bobsvillagers.

"I don't believe it!" said Bob. "Wendy, when did you manage to organise all this?"

"I've had lots of help!" smiled Wendy.

And then everyone cheered, "Hooray for Sunflower Valley!" as fireworks exploded.

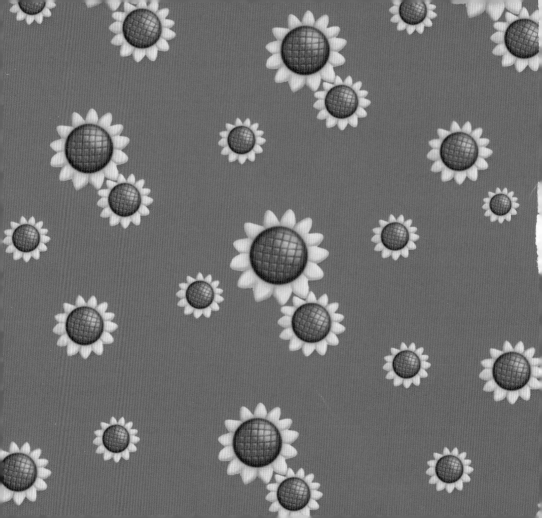

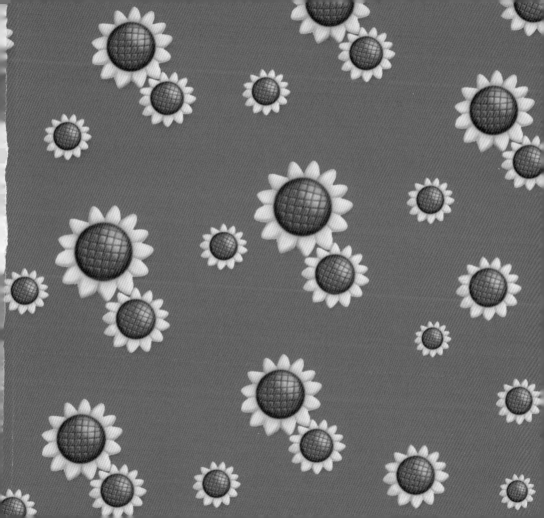